Magical
Mix-Ups

Spells
and
Surprises

First U.S. edition 2014

ISBN 978-0-7636-6610-1

14 15 16 17 18 19 BVG 10 9 8 7 6 5 4 3 2 1

Printed in Berryville, VA, U.S.A.

This book was typeset in Bell MT.
The illustrations were created digitally.

Nosy Crow
an imprint of
Candlewick Press
99 Dover Street
Somerville, Massachusetts 02144

www.nosycrow.com
www.candlewick.com

Magical Mix-Ups

Spells and Surprises

Marnie Edwards * Leigh Hodgkinson

Emerald the Witch

Princess Sapphire

Boris, Emerald's toad

Snowy, Sapphire's cat

Who's Who at St. Aubergine's School

Violet

Nibble, Violet's mouse

Miss Tulip

Add a name here

You'll need these. . . .

Using different tools helps create great drawings.

Use these to add extra SPARKLE and MAGIC.

Sequins

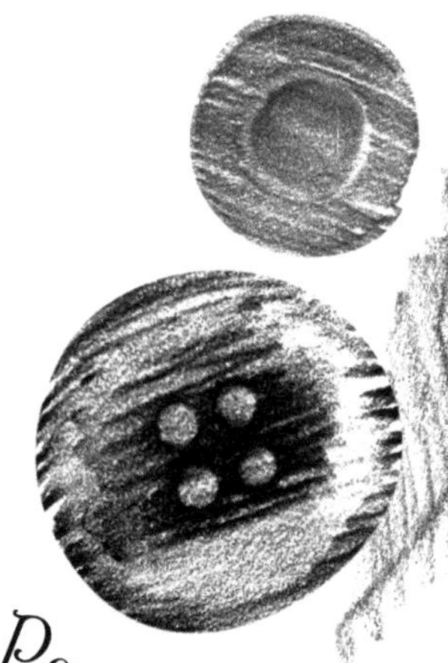

Pencil rubbings

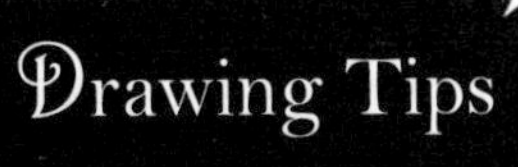

Drawing Tips

Turn to the back of the book for drawing and design ideas!

Tinfoil

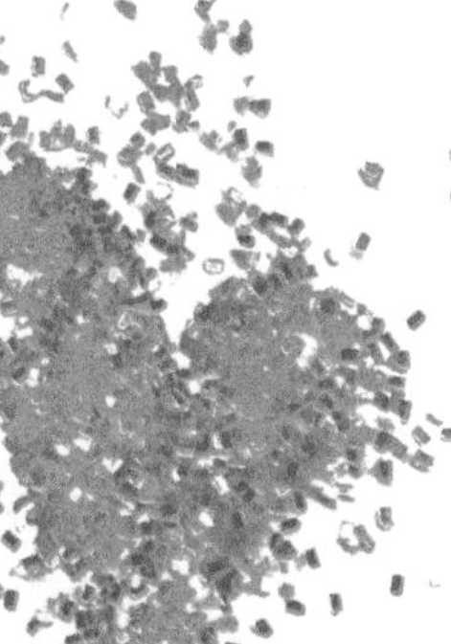

glitter at the READY

GET SET

GO!

Chapter 1

Back to School

Mixtopia is a magical land where everything is out of the ordinary. Princess Sapphire and Emerald the Witch love living there. They also love being best friends!

Add colorful butterflies here.
Add more Mixtopian flowers and trees.

What is the weather like today in Mixtopia?
Look! What is swimming in the river?
Draw a bridge over the river.

One evening, after she has brushed her hair one hundred times, Princess Sapphire gets out her royal diary and pen. In beautiful, curly letters she writes . . .

Spent the day with Em and Boris talking about going to school. VERY EXCITED!

Very important things to do before school starts:

- Buy LOTS of glitter pens
- Choose favorite tiaras (only allowed to take 2 ☹)
- Sew name labels into ALL my lovely dresses

What else is on Sapphire's list?

Draw her favorite dresses and tiaras.
Decorate Sapphire's pencil case.
What else is in here?

Emerald the Witch knows St. Aubergine's Academy will be lots of fun, but she's worried about all the spells she'll have to learn. She's not very good at casting spells.

"I'll just magic up a cake, for practice," she says. "Oops."

Draw more sparks flying out of Emerald's wand.
Show Boris's horrified reaction!

What has Emerald conjured up by accident?

It's time for the friends to pack their trunks. Sapphire squeezes in her ninth tiara and then sits on the lid to close it. Her magical kitten, Snowy, blinks, and both locks snap shut!

Add more shoes and tiaras.
Sapphire
What are these books?
No. 1 PRINCESS DIARIES
Draw a cute little trunk for Snowy.

Pack a spare hat for Emerald.
EMERALD
BIG book of SPELLS
What else do they have to pack?
Add a shiny new wand.
What is in Boris's trunk?
BORIS

The next day, Emerald and Sapphire set off for their new school. They introduce themselves to the other girls on the St. Aubergine's Express.

"I'm Violet," says a girl with springy curls and a mouse on her shoulder. Emerald admires Violet's brand-new broom. It looks really cool, but she seems to be having trouble controlling it.
What is in this lunchbox?
Draw her pet here.

Finish coloring and
decorating this fancy hat.
Whose little
pet is this?

Suddenly, the broom leaps out of Violet's hands and knocks a fancy hatbox to the floor. The hat lands on Boris and covers his eyes. He panics, leaps into the air, and sends everything crashing to the floor.

Who is the owner of this hat?
Who does this lunch box belong to?
Whose tiara is this?
Who does this hair clip belong to?
What a mess!

What does this sign say?
What time is it?
12
1
2
3
4
5
6
7
8
9
10
11
Draw smoke puffing from here
Who is driving the train?

Just as everything has been sorted out, the train pulls into St. Aubergine's Station. The girls have arrived!

Chapter 2
BEDKNOBS
and
broomsticks

The driveway to St. Aubergine's is long and winding, and the school is very grand. Sapphire gulps nervously and holds Emerald's hand.
Add a swirly, curly fence here.
Draw Sapphire's and Emerald's trunks here, please.

Draw more gargoyles.
What are they carrying?
What pet is in here?

Draw the three pets
sitting on the signs.

Emerald decides to magic them to their dormitory, but instead they find themselves in a broom cupboard where Violet is putting away her broomstick.

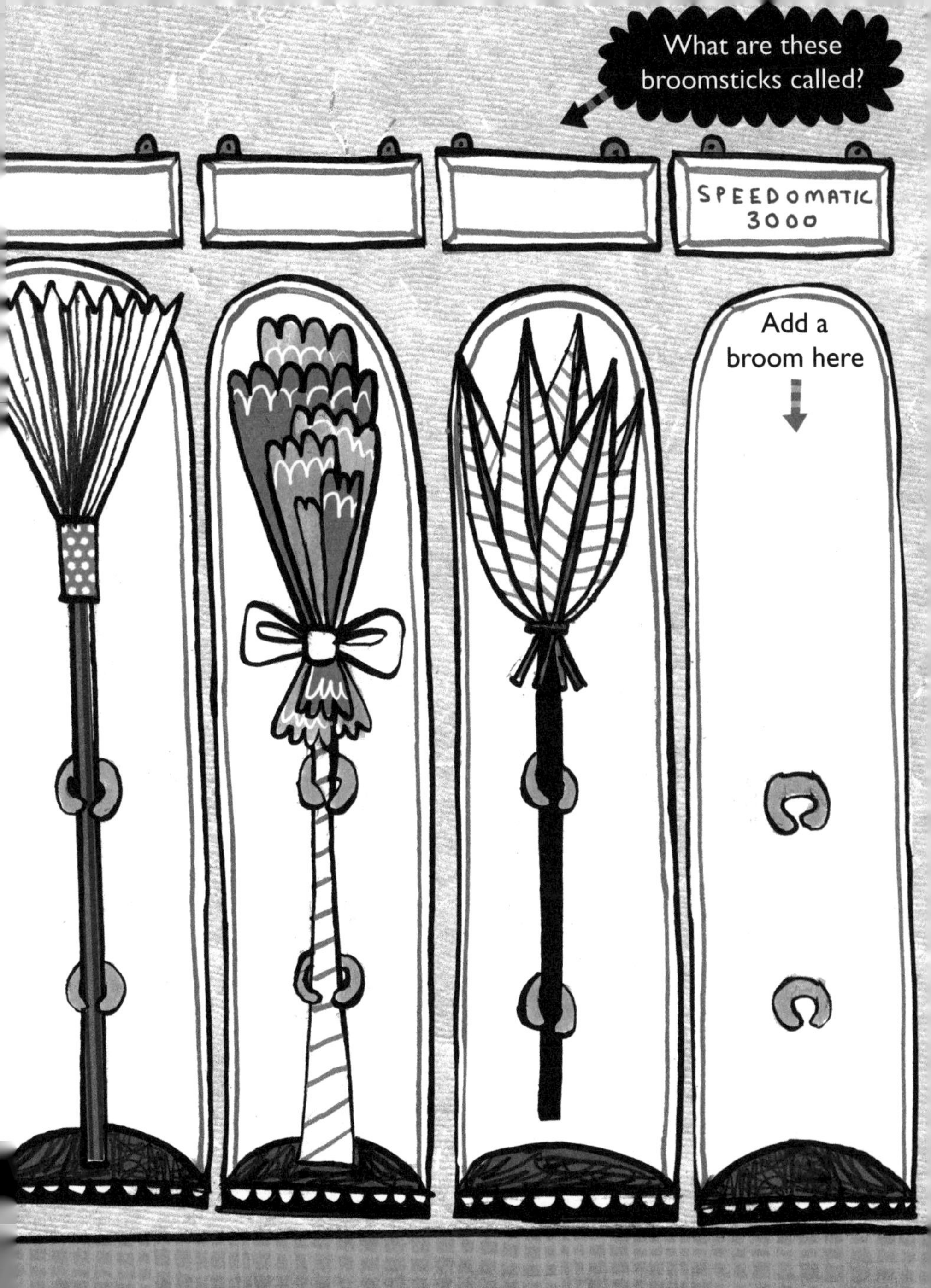

“Oh, hello!” she says, surprised. “Guess what! You’re in my dorm. It’s this way.”

Violet opens the door to a room with three bouncy beds and a sea view. "Oh, look at this beautiful quilt!" says Sapphire. "I call this bed!" Just then, a bell rings for dinner. A green blur heads for the door. . . . Boris is starving!

Draw patterns or attach patterned paper to make pretty quilts.
Whose pictures are in these frames?
Draw a green blur here.

Draw the sea view.
Add pretty curtains, please.
What pictures are in the photo frames?

The hall is filled with chattering girls sitting at long tables that are covered with delicious food. Emerald and Sapphire take their seats just as the headmistress, Miss Tulip, sweeps into the room. "Welcome, everyone!" she cries, beaming.

What is her name?
MISS TULIP, HEADMISTRESS
MISS .... MATH
Add a plate of cinnamon buns here.
Add more yummy food to the table.

Who is sitting here?
What subject does he teach?
MR. SMUDGE,
SCIENCE
Draw flames on the candles.
Who is sitting here?

What is Emerald thinking
about for the festival?

"Exciting news!" says Miss Tulip. "The Halloween Festival is next week! There'll be a Costume Parade! Those of you with broomsticks, I want a display of your skills and daring!" Emerald beams.

"The school must also be decorated from top to bottom," she says. "Get crafty, girls!" Sapphire claps her hands and squeals.

Back in the dorm, the three girls get ready for bed. Emerald is practicing her spells. She picks up her wand, and sparks fly from its tip.

Violet's mouse, Nibble, is suddenly enormous! "Eek!" says Emerald. "RAAAH!" says Nibble.

Violet comes to Emerald's rescue and waves her wand. Nibble is mouse-size again! Emerald sighs sadly. What if she never learns how to cast spells? Could she be the worst witch ever?

Chapter 3

LESSONS

Emerald doesn't feel much better the next morning whe
their teacher Miss Duckling hands out their schedules.

SCHEDULE
name. Sapphire
Add lessons and activities to the schedules.
ON
TUES
WED
THURS
FRI
L
U
N
C
H
etiquette
dancing
FROG kissing
Sing
What does Sapphire have here?
Add funny doodles, please!

Look how many spelling lessons Emerald has!

"And I've got flying," says Violet quietly. "Ooh!" cries Sapphire. "I've got dancing next. Excellent!"

Emerald's already been given her spelling homework. She looks at it and gulps.

Cinderella needs YOUR HELP to get to the BALL! Make up a SPELL that'll turn her PUMPKIN into an AMAZING coach. REMEMBER, it has to rhyme.

Make up a rhyming spell here.

Add lots of decorations.

Mademoiselle Bun, the dance teacher, soon has the princesses whirling around the room while she beats her stick on the floor in time to the music.

Who is playing the piano?

DANCE STUDIO
Give the princesses tiaras.
What shoes is this princess wearing?
Are they wearing tutus or floaty skirts?
Add more twirl lines.
Draw another twirling princess here.

As she glances out the window, Sapphire is sure she sees a curly-haired witch rocket past. . . .

The witch's mouth is open in delight, or maybe terror. Is that Violet?!

Emerald's in her spelling class. She waves her wand carefully over the jar of green gloop in front of her.

Emerald wipes gloop off her hat with Boris's tiny handkerchief. "I hate spelling," she mutters.

At lunchtime, Sapphire notices how sad her friend looks. "What's the matter?" Sapphire asks.

“I can’t cast spells!” says Emerald, sighing. “And there’s a test on Friday. What am I going to do?”

Sapphire and Emerald sit down, and Violet plonks herself next to them. Her hair is full of twigs. “I hate flying,” she mutters.

Chapter 4

Bumps in the night

The next morning, Princess Sapphire is up bright and early. She's so excited about the Halloween Festival! Sapphire is going to make a huge mural for the school hall, using all sorts of natural things she found on the school grounds.

Draw a big pile of pinecones here.
Add leaf rubbings.
Color in using fall colors.

There's so much to get ready!
What is Sapphire holding?
What has Sapphire collected?

Emerald is busy practicing for the witches' flying display and is zooming all over the place. She sees Violet watching her. "Come on up!" she cries.

But Violet just shakes her head sadly.

In art class, everyone has to design Halloween posters—even Boris!

While they work, they tell one another super-spooky stories.

What spooky story is Emerald telling?
Design Boris's poster here.
GLUE

Next, they design their costumes for the parade. Whose will be the scariest?

Draw some scary costume designs here . . .
and another costume here!

Lying awake that night, Emerald hears a loud bump. It seemed to come from the room above. There it goes again! Emerald has goose bumps now. . . .

What on earth could be making that noise?

CRASH!
BANG!
Add more sound effects, please.

Emerald wakes Sapphire and they decide to investigate, with Snowy and Boris right behind them. The intrepid friends stop at the foot of the winding stairs that lead to the turret.

It looks very dark up there. . . .

Give the girls flashlights.

Add more cobwebs and spiders.

BUMP! The noise is getting louder and louder. Could St Aubergine's be HAUNTED?

Chapter 5

TESTING time

They all climb the stairs nervously. Emerald pushes the door open slowly. *CREEAAAK!*

What noise is the ghost making?
Draw a spooky glowing moon here.
Add magical moonlight to the scene.

Give these spiders some scuttle lines.

In the glow of the moonlight, they see a ghostly figure hovering in midair. . . .

Princess Sapphire shrieks with fright, and so does the ghost!
Add some terrified shrieks.
Draw Nibbles's little legs and curly tail poking out.

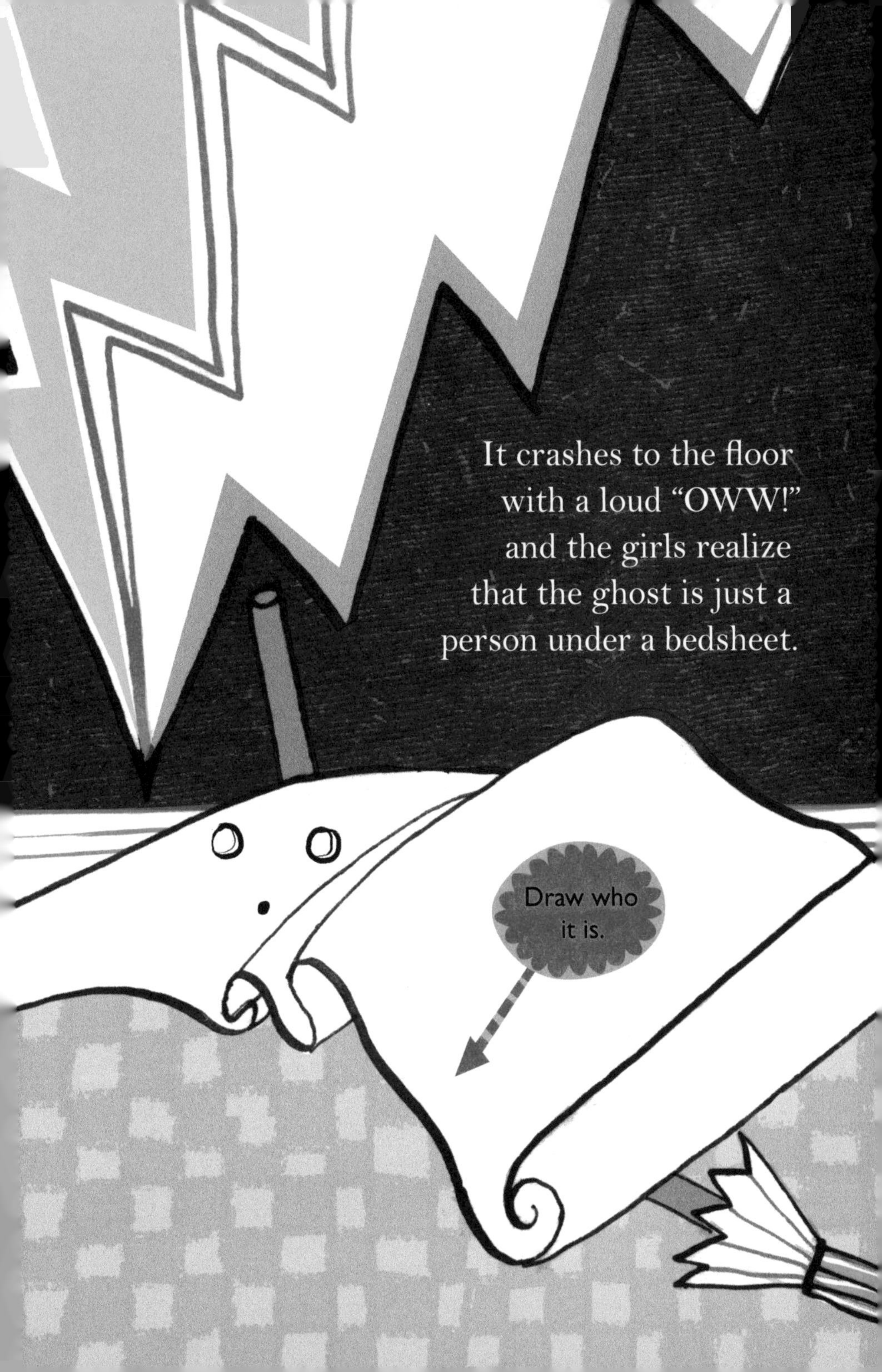

It crashes to the floor
with a loud "OWW!"
and the girls realize
that the ghost is just a
person under a bedsheet.

It's Violet, of course! "I'm practicing for the flying display," she explains, "but I keep falling off. Even my notes don't help. And my costume is getting all dirty!"

Emerald helps Violet to her feet. "I've got an idea!" she says. "I can help you with your flying, and you can help me with my spells!"

"It's a deal!" agrees Violet.

A couple of days later, Emerald stands nervously in front of her spelling class. She points her wand at an apple and says the magic word.

What is written on the blackboard?
Will the apple turn into this?
Or this?
Or this?

The apple turns into a huge pile of candy and marsh-mallows! Just in time to be eaten at the Halloween Festival!

Color in
all the tasty
marshmallows.

Draw more here.
What is Boris about to eat?
Stick wrappers on the sweets to make them sparkle!
Add pieces of cotton balls and glitter.

This time, instead of gloop, Emerald is covered in glory! Emerald's classmates clap and cheer.

Draw a gold medal around her neck.
Fill in Boris's banner.
Who else is on the podium?
1
2
3

Chapter 6

HALLOWEEN

Finally, it's time for the Halloween Festival! The three girls put on their costumes.

What costume does Boris dream he is wearing?
What costume is Snowy dreaming about?
What costume is Nibbles dreaming about?

The school grounds are full of stalls and displays where you can bob for apples, buy spicy Halloween punch, or carve a pumpkin into something hideous!

Draw some magical owls here.
Who else has come to the Halloween Festival?
MAGICAL owl display 1pm
What are the carvings on these pumpkins?
Add a name to this stall.

Everyone loves Sapphire's collage!

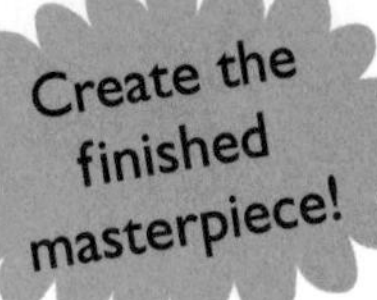
Create the
finished
masterpiece!

Attach autumnal items to give it some WOW!
Draw here.

As dusk falls, it's time for the witches' flying display.

Continue th
loop-the-loo
lines here . .
and here
Add stars to the sky.

Violet loops the loop perfectly, and Emerald casts an amazing spell that makes colored smoke pour out from behind the speeding broomsticks!

Draw Sapphire's shadow here.
Draw Emerald's shadow here.

When the sky is pitch-black,
a huge bonfire is lit and the Costume Parade begins.

The leaping flames cast long shadows behind the spooky figures as they weave about in the eerie light.

Then it's time for toasted marshmallows and singing songs around the fire, while the girls keep warm under a cozy blanket. What a wonderful day!

Add glitter to the stars to make a magical sky.

What are they singing? Write some lyrics here.
Can you add some decorations?

The girls are exhausted after the Halloween Festival, and are soon fast asleep, dreaming up new adventures to have at St. Aubergine's School!
What are they dreaming about?
Finish drawing the pets. Are they asleep or awake?

The Big Picture

Draw your favorite moments from the book, and attach your favorite things.

picture
GLOSSARY
If you need a helping hand thinking of things to draw, then check these ideas out!
wands
fancy bridge
apples
tiaras
yummy cupcakes
spare hats
favorite dresses
St. Aubergine's Express driver

spare
rooms
plates
and
utensils
magic owls
Snowy
Snowy's suitcase
apphire's
pens
pretty
shoes
PERFECT PRINCESS
carved pumpkins
lunch lady
afeteria
food
gargoyles

spiders
Festival decorations
moon and stars
1st Class witch
medal
science teacher
CRASH
sound effects
THU
BAN
pictures for frames
luggage
Halloween costumes